And Then It Happened
..6..

AND THEN IT HAPPENED

·· 6 ··

M & L Wade

Books for Boys

ISBN 0-9731178-5-0

Printed in Canada

Books For Boys
P.O. Box 87
Strathroy ON N7G 3J1

To Reluctant Readers Everywhere

Contents

Chapter 1

The Road Trip

It was the middle of July and Gordon, Paulo and I were bored out of our skulls. School had been out for over two weeks, and except for a day trip to the amusement park, a couple of fishing trips, three summer movies and a trip to the city to see a baseball game, our parents, as usual, had provided us with *nothing* to do. That, however, was about to change. Gordon, Paulo and I had just biked over to Gordon's uncle's house to see the new trailer he just bought. It was a huge 25-foot motor home and was literally a house on wheels. There was a full size bathroom, two bedrooms, a living room, and a kitchen. It had every kind of luxury imaginable.

"Wow, Uncle Ivan!" exclaimed Gordon. "What a great motor home. Where are you going to go with this thing?"

"Well, that's why I invited you three over to have a look at it. Your Aunt Jennifer suggested that we take you and your friends on a trailer trip out west for a couple of weeks. What do you think?" asked Uncle Ivan.

Immediately our faces fell. A two-week trailer trip with Gordon's uncle sounded awesome, but we all knew that our parents would *never* let us be away from home for that long. They'd miss us and worry about us every minute. They would never let us out of their sight for two whole weeks. We sadly explained this fact to Uncle Ivan, making it very clear that we really wanted to go, but that it was probably out of the question.

"That's too bad," replied Uncle Ivan. "I wish I had known that earlier. We invited your parents over tonight to run the idea by them. I was sure they wouldn't mind. They should be here any minute." With that, Uncle Ivan went back into the house to help Aunt Jennifer get ready for their company. Gordon, Paulo and I explored the motor home and admired it.

"This place is better than my house," said Paulo.

"Mine, too," I echoed. "Look at the size of that TV screen!"

"Yeah. It's too bad we can't go on that trip with them," said Gordon, shaking his head. Just then, we noticed our parents arriving. They got out of their cars, stopped briefly to admire the motor home from the outside, and then rang the front doorbell. The door was opened by Aunt Jennifer who invited them all inside.

"Hey, look!" observed Gordon. "The living room window is open. Let's go spy." Quietly, we climbed out of the trailer and scurried across the lawn. We ducked down behind the front bushes and listened to the conversation inside the house. We heard Uncle Ivan explaining that he and Aunt Jennifer wanted to take the three of us out west with them for two weeks. The next thing we heard was the unmistakable sound of glasses clinking together and palms being slapped in high-fives.

"Woo-hoo!" cheered a female voice that sounded

suspiciously like my mother's. Curious, we peered over the window ledge and were surprised to see grins of sheer delight on all of our parents' faces. Gordon's dad raised his arms for silence. When the other adults finally calmed down, he said, "Ivan, I think I speak for all of us when I say that the boys are all yours for the next two weeks. What the heck! Make it three weeks if you like!"

* * * * *

Early the following Saturday morning, we waved good-bye to our families as Uncle Ivan backed the 25-foot motor home out of the driveway and we headed west.

Gordon, Paulo and I carried our duffel bags into one of the bedrooms, and before I realized what was happening, Gordon and Paulo had thrown their duffel bags onto the bunk beds, leaving me with the cheap folding cot. When we finished stowing all of our gear away, we headed up to the front where Uncle Ivan sat in the driver's seat with Aunt Jennifer beside him sorting through some road maps. Uncle Ivan was determined to drive as far as he could on the first day, and he didn't even stop driving when Aunt Jennifer made him a sandwich in the kitchenette for lunch. He ate dinner at the wheel, too. Gordon, Paulo and I passed the time by watching movies on the big screen TV, and when it grew dark out, we headed to our bedroom and soon fell asleep.

Around eleven o'clock, Aunt Jennifer told Uncle Ivan she would take a turn driving. "You've been driving non-stop for fourteen hours. Why don't you go and have a nice hot shower and get a few hours sleep?"

Uncle Ivan stretched and said, "That sounds like a great idea. I am a bit tired." He pulled over long enough to let Aunt Jennifer get behind the wheel and made his way quietly to the bathroom for a long, relaxing shower.

As Aunt Jennifer drove on, she became aware of a tapping sound on the outside of the trailer. The sound didn't stop, and after a few kilometres, she pulled over to the side of the road to investigate. Taking a flashlight, she circled the motor home until she discovered the source of the sound. One of the straps that held our bikes in place had come loose. She quickly fastened it and headed back

5

toward the cab of the motor home. At that same instant, Uncle Ivan emerged from the shower and realized that the motor home was no longer moving. Curious, he glanced around for Aunt Jennifer. Not seeing her anywhere, he grabbed a towel, wrapped it around his waist and stepped out of the back door of the motor home, quietly closing the door behind him so as not to wake Gordon, Paulo and me. And then it happened. At the opposite end of the large motor home, Aunt Jennifer climbed back into the cab, started the engine and took off down the highway, leaving Uncle Ivan stranded by the side of the dark road swatting thirsty mosquitoes and wearing nothing but a towel!

Hour after hour Aunt Jennifer drove on. *"I hope Ivan's having a nice nap,"* she thought. *"He looked awfully tired."*

As Gordon and Paulo slumbered peacefully on their comfortable bunk beds, and I tossed and turned on my cheap cot, I was awakened by the sound of a police siren. It was very close, and Gordon and Paulo awoke, too.

"I'll bet your uncle's speeding!" said Paulo sleepily. The three of us stumbled toward the cab to watch the excitement and were surprised to see Aunt Jennifer behind the wheel, being pulled over by a police car with its lights flashing and siren blaring. The motor home came to a stop. A large policeman approached our motor home and shone a flashlight into the cab. Aunt Jennifer lowered the window, asking, "I'm sorry, Officer. I wasn't speeding, was I?" in her sweetest voice.

"No, ma'am. I pulled you over for an entirely different reason," said the Officer. "You see, I got a naked man in the back of my cruiser who claims he knows you people!"

Gordon, Paulo and I glanced at each other. *A naked man who claims he knows us?* Before Aunt Jennifer or the policeman could stop us, we ran out of the motor home to get a better look at this sicko and tell *him* a thing or two. We rushed toward the police car and pressed our faces against the back window to get a good look for ourselves. We were shocked to see a very angry Uncle Ivan, wrapped in a towel, glaring back at us!

7

"Bedtime, boys!" yelled Gordon, and the three of us high-tailed it back to our bedroom and locked the door, leaving Aunt Jennifer, Uncle Ivan and the policeman to sort things out.

Chapter 2

The Pow Wow

It was the third day of our road trip, and now that we were quite far west, Uncle Ivan had relaxed and was driving for fewer hours each day. We were enjoying the scenery from the comfort of the air-conditioned motor home, and we were able to stop at some of the tourist attractions along the way. As we gazed out the windows at the scenery, a large, colourful sign came into view. It said 'Welcome to the Largest Water Park in the West! 30 km Ahead. Families Welcome!' Before Gordon, Paulo and I had a chance to start chanting, "Let's go to the water park!", Aunt Jennifer noticed a smaller sign.

"West's Best Pow Wow," she read with interest. "Wouldn't that be fun, and educational, too! Ivan, let's take the boys to the Pow Wow." Gordon, Paulo and I looked at each other with dismay. We had learned a long time ago that when someone said, "This will be educational," what they really meant was, "This will be very boring."

"Hey!" said Gordon. "I've got a great idea. Why don't you drop us boys off at the water park and you two can go to the Pow Wow. Then tonight you can tell us all about the educational stuff you saw and we'll tell you about all the fun we had!" Unfortunately Aunt Jennifer failed to see the genius of Gordon's plan, and in a few minutes, we turned off the highway and into the parking lot of the huge Pow Wow. A large sign advertised Native singing, dancing, crafts and music.

"Singing, dancing, crafts and music!" scoffed Gordon. "That sounds just like Kindergarten!"

Uncle Ivan paid our admission and we were introduced to our tour guide, an older Native man dressed in an authentic Native costume.

"Hello," he said. "Today we will show you examples of our singing, dancing, crafts and music." Gordon rolled his eyes. The tour guide frowned at him.

We trailed along as our guide showed us an assortment of ancient Native weapons: clubs, spears, axes, knives and arrow heads, none of which we were allowed to touch. Next, we went into a large teepee that was filled with crafts. Aunt Jennifer oohed and aahed over the beaded moccasins, the dream catchers, and the brightly coloured jewelry. Gordon sighed heavily. Then we were led into a tent where Natives in full traditional costume danced to the beat of a large drum.

"That's kind of cool," I said.

"Yeah, almost as much fun as the Largest Water Park in the West!" said Gordon sarcastically. Our Native guide glared at Gordon and led us to the next attraction. Every time we were shown something new, Gordon found something negative to say about it, and he continued to drop hints about the water park. I'll admit the water park sounded like a lot more fun, but the Pow Wow wasn't that bad.

After several hours at the Pow Wow, we finally came to the end of the tour.

"Now," said our guide. "I don't usually show tourists this last attraction, but I can tell that some of you weren't impressed with our Pow Wow." He glanced at Gordon. "So I'm going to show you one of our most important ancient artifacts. Please come with me."

We followed our guide as he led us to a very old, small teepee. He entered and we heard faint voices inside the tent, and then he opened the flap and motioned our tour group inside. We gathered around our guide. In his hands he held a very worn box. Reaching inside he took out an extremely old pair of moccasins.

"Behold!" said our guide in a serious voice. "The Magic Moccasins!" We all stared at the ancient moccasins, and Gordon let out a loud moan.

"Geez," he grumbled. "I thought this might be something cool, like bows and arrows or spears. Not another pair of old slippers!"

"These are not old slippers!" said our guide sternly. "These moccasins have magic powers."

"Sir," said Gordon. "There is no such thing as magic, and therefore there are no such things as magic moccasins. Nobody believes in silly things like that anymore."

"You are wrong," said our guide patiently. "Any man who wears these moccasins becomes instantly irresistible to women. Women will come from miles around to hug and kiss the man wearing these moccasins. Would anyone like to try them on?"

Uncle Ivan stepped forward and was about to volunteer when Aunt Jennifer pulled him back. "Oh, no you don't!" she said sternly.

"How about you?" said our guide, pointing at Gordon. "I think this young man should try them on and see for himself. Perhaps he will learn not to make fun of our customs and beliefs."

"Those moccasins are not magic!" insisted Gordon.

"Then what harm can come from trying them on? Prove me wrong," our guide dared, holding out the moccasins.

"OK," sighed Gordon. "But don't blame me when nothing happens."

Paulo and I edged closer as Gordon took off his running shoes and slipped into the old moccasins. He stood up and looked at our guide.

"See?" he said. "I told you nothing would happen. Where are all these kissing and hugging women?"

The old man held up his hand. "Just wait," he said quietly. And then it happened. We heard the sound of hundreds of feet pounding on the ground. Like a sudden stampede, it grew closer. The guide lifted up the tent flap and we could see hundreds of men running towards us, their arms outstretched and their lips puckered! The guide glanced down at Gordon's feet and then he shouted,

"Run, you fool! You've got them on the wrong feet!!"

Seeing the crowd of love-struck men running towards

him, Gordon ran for his life. He made it to the far fence in record time and scrambled over it. The men who had been chasing him stopped running and began laughing and slapping each other on the back. Our guide stopped laughing long enough to explain to us what had happened.

"We pull that little joke on everyone who complains as much as that young man did today. I'm sure he's learned a valuable lesson." We all burst into loud laughter.

Still chuckling, Paulo and I took off in search of Gordon before he ran too far away.

Chapter 3

The Magician

We found Gordon hiding in the parking lot outside of the Pow Wow and assured him that the moccasin incident had just been a joke to pay him back for all of his complaining. No one was really chasing him and it was safe to come out. Aunt Jennifer and Uncle Ivan must have been feeling a little guilty because they promised the three of us that we could spend the entire next day at the water park. That cheered Gordon up, and we could hardly wait for morning.

The Wild West Water Park featured water slides, wave pools, inner tube rides, and the world's biggest body slide.

"There's nothing educational here, that's for sure!" said Gordon the next morning as we waited outside the gates for the water park to open.

Gordon, Paulo and I ran through the park, trying every single slide, pool and attraction that the Wild West Water Park had to offer. We were not disappointed. We spent six non-stop hours in 100% pure pleasure, and we happily agreed that we didn't learn a thing. We changed into dry clothes at the end of the day and headed to the parking lot to wait for Aunt Jennifer and Uncle Ivan to pick us up.

As we passed a building with a long line-up on our way out of the park, Paulo said, "Here's something we missed. We didn't go into that building."

"I wonder what everyone is lined up to see," I added.

Gordon spotted the sign over the doorway. "Magic Show," he read. "Well, after that stupid trick yesterday with those fake moccasins, I've decided that I hate magic. It's all fake, anyway. Let's get out of here."

"Wait, Gordon," I said. "Listen. Your aunt and uncle

won't be here for almost an hour. Why wait in a hot parking lot when we can sit in an air-conditioned building and see the show?"

"Yeah," agreed Paulo. "Besides, it was a great water park, so I'll bet this show will be pretty good, too."

"Alright, I'll go, but don't expect me to enjoy it," grumbled Gordon.

We were the last ones in line, and when we entered the building, the only seats left were in the front row where we had to strain our necks and look straight up at the tall stage. Soon the theatre lights dimmed and a single beam of light came on over the stage revealing a magician standing in the centre.

"Welcome," boomed a deep voice. "I am Alakazam the Great. Prepare to be amazed!" The magician took off his hat and bowed deeply to the audience.

"Abracadabra!" he yelled, and a white rabbit appeared suddenly on the top of his head. He hadn't pulled it out of his hat, like magicians usually do. I had to admit, this guy was good. By the look on Paulo's face, he was as surprised as I was. Only Gordon failed to be amused or impressed.

"That's fake!" yelled Gordon. The magician shot Gordon an angry look but continued with his magic show.

"I will now disappear before your very eyes," said Alakazam the Great. There was a loud bang followed by a large puff of smoke. When the smoke cleared, the magician was gone. The audience clapped and cheered, all except Gordon. There was another loud bang and a puff of smoke, and the magician reappeared. Everyone clapped and cheered again.

"There's a trap door in the floor!" shouted Gordon. The magician leered at Gordon.

"Gordon, stop it!" I hissed. "You're going to get us thrown out!"

"Yeah," whispered Paulo. "Shut up or we'll all get in trouble!"

"I don't care. I hate magicians," replied Gordon. "They can't fool me. I know all their tricks."

Every time the magician performed a trick, Gordon would yell out how the trick was done. I could tell that the magician was getting angry, and I expected to be thrown out of the theatre by security guards any second. As he was nearing the end of his show, the magician gave Gordon a sinister looking smile and said, "And now, for my last trick, I will need a volunteer from the audience."

About two hundred hands flew into the air, including mine and Paulo's. Gordon did not raise his hand.

"I will give $20.00 to the person who can stuff this entire handkerchief into his or her mouth while blindfolded!" the magician announced, holding up a large red silk handkerchief.

Suddenly Gordon raised his hand. "I could use twenty bucks!" he said, forgetting that he hated magicians and magic shows.

"Ahhh, how about this young man?" he said, pointing to Gordon. It was more like a command than a question.

"Come up on stage!" ordered the magician, pointing to

the stairs at the side of the stage.

The audience cheered and clapped as Gordon got out of his seat and climbed on stage.

"This isn't fair!" complained Paulo. "Gordon practically ruins this guy's magic show, and then he gets to go up on stage and win twenty bucks!"

On stage, the magician was asking Gordon his name.

"Gordon Smith," said Gordon in a loud, confident voice.

"Well, Gordon," said the magician, holding up the red handkerchief. "Do you think you can fit this entire handkerchief in your mouth for $20.00? I'm pretty sure your mouth is big enough!" The audience laughed.

"I know I can," bragged Gordon, ignoring the magician's insult. "This is the easiest $20.00 I've ever made."

"We shall see about that," said the magician mysteriously. He grinned at the audience.

The magician tied a blindfold around Gordon's eyes. Once he was sure Gordon couldn't see anything, he held

21

up the red handkerchief for the audience once again. And then it happened. The magician quickly put the handkerchief in his front pocket and reached around to his back pocket and produced a pair of red silk underwear! The audience gasped and laughed. Gordon mistook this for cheering and he smiled and waved at the crowd.

The magician handed the red underwear to Gordon, who immediately began cramming them into his mouth. The audience roared with laughter at the sight of a kid stuffing underwear into his mouth. His cheeks bulged but he managed to get the whole pair into his mouth. The audience went wild with laughter and applause. Gordon took a bow before taking what he thought was just a handkerchief out of his mouth. The magician took the underwear from Gordon and held them up one last time before putting them in his back pocket, then quickly pulled out the real handkerchief from his front pocket. He untied Gordon's blindfold and handed him a twenty dollar bill that he produced out of thin air. The audience broke into thunderous applause.

"See?" said Gordon as he returned to his seat. "Nothing to it. And I'm twenty bucks richer!"

I glanced at Paulo. Should we tell Gordon the truth, or let him enjoy his money? Then I got an idea.

"Gordon," I said. "I know something about that trick that *you* don't know."

"What?" he asked.

"It'll cost you," I said.

"What do you mean? It was just a dare. That magician didn't think I could fit that whole handkerchief into my mouth, and I did. That's not even a real trick!"

"For ten dollars, I'll tell you what really happened, *if you want to know*," I suggested mysteriously.

"Nothing happened," said Gordon defensively. "You're just trying to get my money." He didn't sound completely sure of himself, though.

"Ask Paulo if you don't believe me," I said.

"It's true," agreed Paulo. "Something happened on that stage that made you look like a fool. But it will cost you ten dollars to get me to tell you."

"What?" yelled Gordon. "If I pay both of you guys ten dollars, that will leave me with exactly nothing!"

"I guess you'll never know what really happened on that stage, then," I said, and Gordon never did find out the truth.

Chapter 4

Meow Mix-Up

It was a hot summer day and Gordon, Paulo and I had been sent to the grocery store to buy ice cream for a large party that Gordon's mother was giving that afternoon. We paid for the ice cream and were about to leave when Gordon stopped at the community message board – the place where people put up notices about lost pets or things for sale. One particular ad caught Gordon's eye.

"Look at this," he said. The ad read:

"Responsible Person Needed to Babysit Cat for 3 Days. $30.00."

Beneath the typing was a picture of a large black cat

with the caption "Whiskers."

"I know that cat," said Gordon. "His owner lives about five doors down from our house. I wonder why he didn't ask me to look after his cat. Heck, I'm responsible."

"Because Chopper would probably eat the cat," I said, thinking back to an unfortunate incident involving a gerbil entrusted to Gordon's 'responsible' care. Gordon gave me a nasty look but didn't say anything. The three of us hurried off to Whiskers' house to talk with the owner.

When we arrived at the house, Mr. O'Brien, Whiskers' elderly owner, was out front cutting his lawn. He shut off the mower when he saw us coming up the driveway. Gordon got right to the point.

"Hi, Mr. O'Brien. We saw your ad at the grocery store and your worries are over. We will take excellent care of Whiskers. We like cats, and we sure could use thirty bucks."

I could immediately see that Mr. O'Brien was not

thrilled at the idea of the three of us taking care of his cat.

"Well," he stammered. "I was hoping that someone a little older might want the job. Whiskers is very, very important to me. He's all I've got and, well, to be honest, I've heard a lot of stories about you three."

Setting the grocery bag of ice cream down on the hot driveway, Gordon proceeded to tell Mr. O'Brien how we were actually very responsible young men and that the stories he had heard about us had been greatly exaggerated.

Mr. O'Brien wasn't convinced. "I wanted someone a little older," he said again.

"Older than us?" said Gordon. "But think about it, Mr. O'Brien. If you add our ages together, we're very old. Probably as old as you." Gordon thought for a moment. "Well, maybe not *that* old, but if you hire us, you'll get *three* responsible people instead of just one for the same price."

Mr. O'Brien threw his hands up in defeat. "OK, OK. I'll hire you boys. Besides, no one else has applied for the job and I leave on my trip in two days, so I'm kind of desperate. Come on in and I'll show you where everything is."

We followed Mr. O'Brien into the back yard so he could show us where he hid the house key that unlocked the back door. We then entered the house and went down the basement steps. Whiskers lay sleeping on an old chair. The large black cat opened his eyes to look us over and then yawned and went back to sleep. Gordon, Paulo and I took turns petting Whiskers, who purred loudly in his sleep.

"Boy," I thought. *"This is going to be the easiest $30.00 we ever made."*

Next, Mr. O'Brien led us to the furnace room and showed us the litter box and cat dishes. The instructions were simple. Once a day, we were to come over and put fresh water in the water dish and open a can of cat food and put it in the food dish. Whiskers was an indoor cat, and we were to make sure he didn't get outside.

As we left the house, we assured Mr. O'Brien that with

three responsible kids like us on the job, he had nothing to worry about. Gordon picked up the dripping bag of ice cream from the hot driveway and we hurried home to deliver it to his mother.

*   *   *   *   *

Two days later, Gordon Paulo and I headed over to Mr. O'Brien's house to check on Whiskers. The key was right where the old man had shown us, and we found the cat sleeping on his chair in the basement. He opened his eyes, looked us over, yawned and went back to sleep.

"It's like taking candy from a baby," said Gordon. "Imagine what we can buy with $30.00!"

We went into the furnace room and put fresh water in the cat's dish and opened a can of cat food. I gave Whiskers an affectionate scratch behind the ear and we left the house, locking up behind us. We carefully put the key back in its hiding spot.

The next day was a repeat of the first. We entered the house, found Whiskers asleep in the basement, petted him, fed him, put out fresh water and left.

On our third and last day, we entered the house and went through the same routine.

"Whew!" said Paulo as we filled the cat's food and water dishes. "That litter box smells worse than the pig pen at my farm. Whatever you do, don't take the lid off it."

"Let's show Mr. O'Brien how responsible we are," said Gordon. "Let's air out the place a bit before he gets back today."

He went over to the window and opened it to let in a fresh breeze. "That's better," he said.

We locked up the house and went around to the back yard to put the key back in its hiding place. Hearing a sound behind us, we turned around just in time to see a large black object leap out of the open basement window and streak across the yard into the bushes!

"Oh, no!" I yelled. *"Whiskers has escaped!"*

The three of us raced towards the bushes and immediately began calling the cat, but no amount of coaxing could make him come out of his hiding place.

"He could be anywhere by now," said Paulo. "And he's an indoor cat, so he's bound to get lost in the neighbourhood."

"Thanks for the cheerful thought," said Gordon sarcastically. "What are we gonna do? The old man's due back in three hours!"

"I knew it was too easy," I sighed, picturing a long, hot afternoon searching for the cat. "If we don't find Whiskers, we won't get paid."

We jumped on our bikes and began combing the neighbourhood for Whiskers. We called and whistled for what seemed like hours. We crawled through bushes and hedges and peered over people's fences. Finally, about two hours later, Paulo spotted the cat crossing a street. We pedalled furiously after him. Sensing that he was being chased, Whiskers put on a burst of speed. He darted between parked cars and we lost sight of him for a moment.

"There he is!" cried Gordon, pointing up a tall tree. Perched on a branch about halfway up was Whiskers, his black fur gleaming in the sun. Gordon climbed the tree, talking softly to the cat. When he got within an arm's reach, the once-docile Whiskers hissed and clawed at Gordon. Now that he had tasted freedom, the cat was not going back to the basement without a fight.

All of a sudden I got an idea. Calling up to Gordon, I said, "You and Paulo wait here and guard the cat. I'll be right back." I jumped on my bike and pedalled home. I returned a few minutes later with a large pillowcase.

"Here," I said, handing it to Paulo, who had climbed the tree to help Gordon. I was relieved to see that Whiskers was still on the branch. Together, Gordon and Paulo managed to get the cat into the pillowcase, but not before he put up one heck of a fight. Both boys were scratched and sweaty by the time they climbed out of the tree with Whiskers securely in the pillowcase. Whiskers was yowling and hissing and thrashing about, and it was a challenge to carry him home on our bikes.

We got to Mr. O'Brien's house, unlocked the door and carried the cat, still in the pillowcase, down to the

32

basement.

"Quick! Close that window," said Paulo. Gordon quickly shut the window and I let Whiskers out of the pillowcase. He took off like a shot and hid under his chair, no doubt angry at us for spoiling his fun. We locked up and put the key back in its hiding spot.

"Thank goodness that's over!" I sighed. "This is the hardest $30.00 I've ever earned!"

Exhausted from our efforts of the day, we rode back to Gordon's house and relaxed on his front porch, sipping cold drinks and waiting for Mr. O'Brien to return from his vacation and pay us our money.

Right on time, the old man pulled into his driveway. Getting out of his car, he walked over to Gordon's house and asked us how everything had gone.

"Did Whiskers give you boys any trouble?" he asked.

"None at all," lied Gordon.

"He was as good as gold," added Paulo.

Mr. O'Brien eyed the scratches on Gordon and Paulo suspiciously but said nothing. Taking out his wallet, he counted out three crisp ten dollar bills and handed one to each of us.

"Thank you very much, boys," he said.

"Thank you," we chorused.

"I'm very tired from my trip," said the old man. "I'm going straight home to bed." He turned around and went back home, waving to us from his driveway.

"Now," said Gordon, his old energy returning. "How shall we spend our cash?"

"I say we go to the corner store and buy snacks with it!" suggested Paulo.

"Lots of candy!" I added. "I'm starving after all that running around this afternoon."

Forty five minutes later we sat on the curb by the corner store with our empty candy bags around us.

"Man, I'm stuffed!" said Paulo, rubbing his stomach.

"I ate way too much," moaned Gordon.

I opened my mouth to shove in the last piece of my candy when I suddenly spied a cat sitting under a bench in the park across the road – a black cat. A cat that looked an awful lot like Whiskers!

"Uh-oh!" I said. "Gordon, didn't you close that window in the basement?"

"Yeah. I'm positive I closed it. Why?"

Then Paulo caught sight of the cat and pointed across the street. "Wow. That cat looks just like Whiskers."

Hearing his name, the cat trotted over to us. He purred and rubbed against our legs like a long-lost friend. An odd feeling crept over me.

"Guys," I said in a quiet voice. "Are you thinking what I'm thinking?"

"Yup," said Paulo.

"Yup," said Gordon. "Mr. O'Brien went home and smelled that litter box. He opened the window to air out the basement and Whiskers got out again."

"**No, you dummy!**" I practically shouted. "Whiskers has been out here all along. The cat we caught in the tree was some other black cat. *We put the wrong cat in the old man's basement!*"

"What are we going to do now?" moaned Gordon.

"I guess we'll have to take the real Whiskers back to Mr. O'Brien's house and confess what happened," said Paulo.

"Oh, jeez," moaned Gordon, rolling his eyes. "We told him we were responsible and that he had nothing to worry about. If he knows we let his cat out, he'll want his money back, and we've spent it all. No, here's what we're going to do. We know where Mr. O'Brien keeps his spare key. We'll just sneak into the house quietly while he's sleeping and switch cats. The old man will never know."

The plan sounded good. Paulo picked up the purring Whiskers and we hurried over to Mr. O'Brien's house. We ran around to the back yard to get the key, but when we looked in the usual hiding spot, it wasn't there.

"Oh, no," I sighed. "Mr. O'Brien must have taken the key out of the hiding spot now that he's back home."

"I know!" said Gordon. "That basement window I opened this morning didn't have a lock on it! We can crawl through it and switch cats!"

Gordon ran over to the window and gently opened it.

The opening was just wide enough for Gordon to crawl through.

Fortunately for us, the other cat was asleep on Whiskers' chair, no doubt tired from his ordeal earlier today. Gordon snuck up on the cat and grabbed him tightly before he knew what hit him. He carried the struggling cat to the window and released the wild cat into the backyard. The cat tore off across the yard and disappeared under the fence.

"Good riddance," I muttered.

Paulo gently handed Whiskers to Gordon, who placed the purring cat on his chair. And then it happened.

Gordon clutched his stomach in pain. "Ohhh!" he moaned.

"Gordon, what's the matter?" whispered Paulo, worried.

"Cramps," groaned Gordon. "Bad ones. I ate too much candy."

"It was all that pop," I said, not feeling too well myself.

"I need a bathroom real bad," whispered Gordon.

"Come on. We'll pull you through the window and you can run home," said Paulo.

"*No time*," said Gordon, frantically dancing around the dark basement.

"Well, you can't go upstairs! The old man will hear you!" I hissed.

Suddenly Gordon ran full speed into the furnace room. I heard him remove the lid to the cat's litter box and set it down on the concrete. Paulo heard it, too, and we stared at each other in disbelief. Gordon was using Whiskers' litter box!!

We heard a long sigh and several minutes later, looking much better, Gordon reappeared. He tiptoed over to the window and Paulo and I quickly pulled him out. We quietly shut the window and without a backward glance, we raced for home.

I promised myself that I would never babysit a cat with Gordon again, no matter how much the job paid.

Chapter 5

The Sunglasses

This morning, something very funny happened to Gordon. At least, Paulo and I thought it was funny, and so did my mom. Gordon didn't think it was funny at all. Here's what happened. You be the judge.

Gordon's parents had bought him a really cool pair of sunglasses, and not just cheap kiddie ones, either. These were the real deal. They had very dark lenses and were very expensive. Naturally, Gordon wanted to show them off to Paulo and me, and so Paulo and I were waiting in my backyard for Gordon to show up and start bragging. I wanted my mom to see the sunglasses so that I could start bugging her for a pair, too. I figured it was never too soon to start pestering your parents for something you really wanted. I knew she would cave in after a couple of weeks of sincere begging.

Paulo showed up right on time, but Gordon was late. This was odd because Gordon was almost never late, especially when he had the chance to show off. An hour went by with no sign of Gordon. After another 30 minutes passed, Paulo and I decided that Gordon must have been in a serious bike accident and was lying in a ditch, unconscious and bleeding. We thought that we'd better get on our bikes and go looking for him. Just as we were about to bike off, my mom announced that lunch was ready. Well, first thing after lunch we would go and look for Gordon.

As Paulo and I started in on our second helping of blueberry pie, Gordon knocked on the door. My mom opened it.

"Gordon," I said through a mouthful of pie. "You're late. We were really worried."

"What happened to you?" asked Paulo, noticing the

strange look on Gordon's face, as if something bad had just happened.

"Where are your new sunglasses?" I added.

Gordon reached into his back pocket and handed me a case containing the new sunglasses.

"Here," he said woefully. "They're all yours. I don't want them anymore." He shuddered deeply. "I'll never wear sunglasses again as long as I live!"

"Why? What happened?" asked Paulo curiously.

Gordon sat down at our kitchen table. "Oh, it was horrible, just horrible!" he said, staring blankly into space.

"Gordon! What happened?" I asked, beginning to get a little alarmed.

"Oh, the horror! The horror!" he moaned dramatically.

"Gordon, what happened?" shouted my mom, snapping Gordon out of his trance. My mom enjoyed a good Gordon story as much as the rest of us. We all sat on the edge of our seats, anxious to hear what trouble Gordon had gotten himself into this time.

"Well," began Gordon, taking a deep breath. "A

41

couple of hours ago, I left my house to come over here to show you my new sunglasses. About two blocks from home, I came across this man lying on the sidewalk. He was blind and I could tell he was injured. His seeing-eye dog was sitting beside him. Naturally, I asked if he needed help. He moaned and said that he had been on his way to deliver a package. There was a box lying near him. He had tripped on a loose piece of sidewalk, and his ankle looked pretty swollen. 'Do you want me to call an ambulance?' I asked, all concerned. *'No,'* he said, pointing up the street. *'I just live over there. If you could help me home, I'll put some ice on my ankle, and if it doesn't get any better, I'll call my doctor. "*

Gordon stopped for a deep breath and then continued. "So I picked up the man's package and helped him to his feet. His dog stayed real close and guided us to his house. When we got to his front door, he said, *Thanks a lot, young man. I'll be OK from here, but can I ask you for one more small favour?'* 'Sure,' I said. 'How can I help?'

'Well, I was wondering if you could deliver this package

for me. The address is on the front, and it's not too far.'
'No problem,' I said. 'I'd be happy to.' *'Oh, just one more thing, '* he added as I was turning to go. *'Would you mind taking my dog along for some exercise? I won't be able to walk him for a while with this ankle and he needs regular exercise. His name's Jake, '* he said. He thrust the harness in my direction and so I said, 'Sure, no problem. Come on, Jake!' And we set off. I never imagined how it must have looked – me in my dark sunglasses walking a seeing-eye dog! Anyway, fifteen minutes later I found the house and rang the doorbell, but there was no answer. I rang it again, but there was still no answer. I couldn't see a mailbox to put the package into, so I rang the doorbell one more time. This time, a window on the second floor opened and this really old lady stuck her head out and yelled, *'Oh, there you are! I was just in the shower. I'll be right down.'* She was at the door within seconds, and then it happened." Gordon shuddered again.

"Go on," urged my mom.

"Well, the door flew open, and there stood the old lady,

wearing nothing but her birthday suit! That's when it hit me. *She thought I was blind!!* Well, before I knew what was happening, she grabbed me by the wrist and pulled me and Jake into the house, gushing all over me.

'Oh, you poor thing! They said a blind man was going to deliver this package, but you're just a boy!' On and on she went. Well, I didn't dare take off my sunglasses or tell her the truth! I just kept my eyes scrunched up so tight they hurt. I bumped into things, but that just made it more believable. She insisted on making me sit down at the kitchen table and eat lunch! *I just spent the last hour and a half with somebody's 90 year old naked grandmother!!*"

Paulo, my mom and I shrieked with laughter. Gordon stared at the floor, shaking his head.

"An hour and a half with my eyes clenched shut for dear life," he murmured. "I couldn't wait to get out of there. I swear I will *never* wear sunglasses again!"

Chapter 6

The Test

I don't know who hates parent-teacher interviews more – the kids, because we're worried about what our teachers might say to our parents that will get us into trouble; the teachers, because they're worried about what they might say that will get *themselves* into trouble; or the parents, who have heard it all before and resigned themselves to the fact that they're not raising the next Einstein. Even the custodians hate parent-teacher interviews because they've got to spend dozens of extra hours making sure that the school is spotless and shining.

It was the day of parent-teacher interviews at

Danglemore Public School. Interviews were set to begin right after school and our class had spent the last period of the day tidying up the room so that our parents would think it was always this neat. Everyone had a job to do. Paulo had to wash the blackboards, Gordon had to clean out the hamster cage, and I had to empty the garbage cans. We all had to clean out our desks and wash the tops, a chore which took Gordon quite a while because his desk was especially cluttered.

When the bell rang at the end of the day, we were all happy to go home and get some rest.

"Man, those garbage cans really stink!" I complained.

"Well, cleaning the blackboards is no fun, either," grumbled Paulo.

"And that hamster cage..." began Gordon, his voice trailing off. "On, no!" he moaned. "Mrs. H. is gonna kill me! I forgot to clean out the hamster cage!"

"Well, there's my bus," said Paulo. "I gotta go. Sorry about your luck, Gordon." And with that, Paulo quickly climbed aboard the waiting bus.

"Come on," said Gordon, grabbing me by the arm.
"We've got to go back and clean that cage."

"What do you mean 'we'? You're the one who forgot!
I did *my* job."

"It'll be faster with two of us," Gordon insisted.
"Besides, Mrs. Hoagsbrith likes you. She won't be so mad
if she sees you with me."

I sighed and followed Gordon back into the school.
The halls were deserted. We made our way to the second
floor and peered into our classroom. It, too, was empty.

"Whew! We're in luck. She's not here. Let's get this
over with and get out before she even knows I forgot."
Gordon quickly set to work cleaning the hamster's cage,
and then it happened. Just as he was putting the hamster
back into his clean cage, we heard our teacher's voice in
the hall and froze. She was laughing and talking to some
parents and coming closer every second.

"Quick! Hide!" hissed Gordon.

"Where?" I asked, looking around the room.

"Under there!" ordered Gordon, pushing me under the

teacher's big wooden desk just as Mrs. Hoagsbrith and two parents entered the room.

"Oh, no!" mouthed Gordon as we both recognized *his* parents' voices. Mr. And Mrs. Smith sat down in front of the teacher's desk and our teacher perched on top facing them. We could see her shoes and ankles dangling just inches from our faces.

"Well," began Mrs. Hoagsbrith. "I like to start every interview off on a positive note. I'm pleased to tell you that your son is a very honest boy. With marks as low as his, I just know he's not cheating!"

Gordon scowled as the three adults chuckled. As the interview continued, my legs began to cramp up, but I didn't dare move, and I prayed that Mrs. Hoagsbrith stayed where she was, too.

"Although Gordon's grades are average, I really feel that he is a very bright student. If he just paid more attention in class and completed his homework assignments on time, I believe he could get top marks. He's got a great deal of potential. In fact, Gordon may be one of the brightest students I've taught in 25 years. With your permission, I would like Gordon to take a test to determine just how smart he really is. There are special classes that would challenge him and help him live up to his true potential."

Judging by the silence in the room, Mr. and Mrs. Smith didn't know what to make of this news. Was Mrs. Hoagsbrith serious? I glanced at Gordon. Could he really be a genius?

"Well," said Mrs. Smith at last. "I think it would be good for Gordon to take that test."

"I agree," said his father, a note of pride in his voice. Under the desk, Gordon's face fell. Clearly he did not think the test would be good for him.

When the interview was finally over and the adults had left the room, Gordon and I crawled stiffly out from under the desk.

"I'm not taking that test!" said Gordon firmly, stamping his foot to wake it up. "If they find out I'm smart, they'll just make me work twice as hard. I'm happy being average, thank you very much."

We snuck out of the building and rode our bikes over to Paulo's house to tell him what we had overheard.

"And I always thought *you* were the smart one," I said to Paulo. "Who would have thought it would turn out to be Gordon?"

"Hey!" said Gordon, insulted. "Anyway, Paulo can go right on being the smart one. I'm going to fail that test on purpose. Did you hear what Mrs. H. said about special classes and working harder? I don't even want to do half the work she assigns now!"

A few days later, Gordon was pulled out of class and sent to the library to take the special test. He was gone for quite a while, and I kept glancing at Paulo the whole time.

"I'll bet Gordon's having fun trying to fail that test on purpose," I said at recess.

When we filed back into class after the bell rang, Gordon was sitting in his desk. He turned and gave us the thumbs up and a big smile.

"There's no way anyone will think I'm a genius now,"

he said with satisfaction after school that day. We were
sitting in my tree fort and Gordon was telling us all about
the test.

"I knew most of the answers, so maybe Mrs. H. was
right and I am a genius, but I made sure I failed that test
good. Extra work!? Special classes!? What was she
thinking?"

*   *   *   *   *

Two days later, Mrs. Hoagsbrith called Gordon's
parents for a special meeting to discuss the test.

"I'm really surprised," she told them. "I was certain
that he was a lot smarter than his marks in class indicate,
but, well...see for yourselves." She passed Gordon's test
paper across her desk. Mrs. Smith gasped when she saw
the grade. Mr. Smith cleared his throat. Neither one said
a word as they stared at the big red 'F' at the top of the
page.

"I guess I was wrong about Gordon being so clever,"
said Mrs. Hoagsbrith. "It's obvious he had some real
difficulties with this test. He had trouble answering even

the most basic questions." The teacher cleared her throat and said, "What I'm recommending is that Gordon be given some extra work and special help before school, at recess and after school, plus perhaps a tutor on Saturday mornings until we get him caught up to where he should be. I'm sure that with a lot of extra work, Gordon can catch up in just a few months."

"Of course," said Mr. Smith. "We'll do whatever it takes to help our son, even if it means sending him to summer school!"

Chapter 7

The Haunted House

On the edge of our town there is an old house that has been abandoned for years. When we were younger, Gordon's dad told us many stories about the house. He said that the house was possessed and any kids that entered it NEVER came out again. To prove this, Gordon's dad would point out how there were fewer kids around these days and he said it was because they had gone into the abandoned house.

Of course, now that we were older, we knew that the house wasn't really haunted. Gordon's dad had just told us all those stories to keep us from playing near the house, which was dangerous because it was old and falling apart.

It was Gordon who decided that it was time we finally explored this long-abandoned house and Paulo and I agreed. Even though we didn't *really* believe the house was possessed or even haunted, we had all seen enough horror movies to know that when you explored an old house, you had better come prepared for the worst, just in case. Naturally, we had a plan.

Setting out for the abandoned house the following day, we carried flashlights and about 10 metres of heavy rope. The plan was to tie the rope around Gordon's waist and let him climb through a broken basement window that we had discovered. We figured Gordon could prowl around the basement and if anything happened to him, he could yell or yank on the rope and Paulo and I would pull him back up through the window.

Arriving at the house, Gordon climbed down through the broken basement window and swept his flashlight around the room. Seeing nothing dangerous, he began to explore. Outside, Paulo and I fed him more and more rope as Gordon ventured further into the basement. A couple of minutes passed, and then the thing that Paulo and I had been dreading happened. We felt two frantic jerks on the rope, our signal that Gordon was in trouble! We immediately began to haul on the rope, pulling him back towards the window. We could feel his body bouncing off of doorframes and walls as we pulled him to safety.

Suddenly, out of the darkness of the basement, a headless human body appeared. Paulo and I shouted and jumped back from the window, and then we laughed as we realized that it was only an old store mannequin.

Gordon's own body popped up from the basement window. "Gotcha, didn't I?" he laughed. "I found our friend here in the furnace room. There's all kinds of great stuff down here. Come on!"

Turning on our flashlights, Paulo and I lowered ourselves into the basement and followed Gordon. The basement was damp and musty. There was water in one corner from last night's rain. Old broken-down furniture was scattered about the floor, gnawed at by mice or rats.

There were rusty tools, old tires and cans of paint. Everything was covered in cobwebs.

We shone our flashlights on the stairs and cautiously climbed to the first floor, carefully testing our weight on each step as we went. Because most of the windows had been boarded up, the main floor of the house was almost as dark as the basement. In the kitchen, bits of broken dishes crunched under our feet. The kitchen table had been knocked over. Laying next to it were two broken chairs. The rest of the house was just as bad. There were moldy beds covered in moth-eaten sheets, holes in the walls and piles of junk everywhere. Upstairs, the attic was the same – dark and cluttered. There were trunks of old clothes, dusty books and magazines, and a large mirror on a stand. Propped up in a corner was a huge portrait of a sinister-looking man with a beard staring straight ahead.

"Hey, look at this," said Paulo. "This guy's eyes seem to follow you when you move around the room!"

That gave Gordon an idea. "Hey! You know how our

school is trying to raise money for charity this Halloween? Well, I'll bet we could make a really great haunted house here and charge admission!" he said. "Our class will raise a ton of money and we would win that pizza party for sure!"

"That's a great idea," I said. "But there's one small problem. This house isn't ours. In fact, we're not even supposed to be here right now."

"You're right," agreed Paulo. "We wouldn't even be able to advertise our haunted house."

"That's even better," exclaimed Gordon. "It'll be a *secret* haunted house. Word will spread through school and everyone will want to come!"

It was a great idea, and we got to work on it right away. We worked after school and all day on Saturday getting our haunted house ready. Gordon, Paulo and I decided that our haunted house would not be your average, run-of-the-mill haunted house, with witches, tombstones and glowing pumpkins. We figured that kids had seen enough of that over the years, and we wanted *our* haunted house to be unlike any other. The house was pretty spooky by itself, and with a few simple changes, we could make it a terrifying but fun experience for everyone.

Word spread quickly at school, and every day at recess kids talked excitedly about our haunted house.

"Admission is one dollar, and it's for charity," Gordon reminded everyone. "Remember to bring a flashlight and come in through the basement window around back."

Finally it was Halloween, and we were all set to go. With a can of red paint that we found in the basement, we had made a trail of bloody footprints for the kids to follow through the house. Paulo sat outside the basement window, collecting money in a large jar, and I sat under the stairs, waiting for the first kid to drop through the window into the basement.

I saw a pair of legs appear, followed by the rest of a boy's body as our first client entered our haunted house. Dropping into the spooky basement, he shone his flashlight around. One of the rats that lived in the basement ran by the boy and squealed. The boy gulped in fear. Spotting the fake bloody footprints, he started following them, swinging his flashlight back and forth into the shadows as he walked slowly towards the stairs. He spotted some spider webs, and thinking that they were fake, he brushed them aside. He quickly jerked his arm back as the real spider that lived in the web scurried towards his hand. Reaching the steps, the boy cautiously began to climb them. Just as his foot reached the fifth step, I reached out and grabbed his ankle. The kid screamed and ran the rest of the way up the stairs, where Gordon was hiding, waiting...

When the boy caught his breath at the top of the stairs and was certain that nothing was slithering up the steps after him, he shone his flashlight around the kitchen. The trail of bloody footprints led him to the living room and stopped in front of a large window. On the wall over the window was a message that looked like it had been written in blood:

Beware

Of

being

pushed

Out

of

the

window.

As the words got smaller, the boy leaned closer and closer to the wall in order to read the message we had written in red paint. Reading the words out loud, he was unaware that Gordon was sneaking up behind him. Just as he finished the message, Gordon pushed the boy through the open window! The boy yelled as he fell, headfirst. He landed safely on a thick pile of old musty mattresses that we had found in the bedroom. He sat up and laughed as he realized that we had just played a great joke on him.

It was nearing eight o'clock, and the haunted house had been a huge success. Some kids were too scared to make it out of the basement, and Paulo had to lower a ladder for them to climb back out, but many kids came through two and three times. The jar was overflowing with money and everything seemed to be going smoothly, and then it happened.

A policeman driving by the abandoned house on his usual rounds noticed some movement in the backyard and decided to investigate. He pulled his car to a stop in front of the house, and seeing the lights of the cruiser, there was an instant stampede as kids tore off in all directions. Paulo grabbed the money jar and jumped through the basement window.

"Quiet!" he hissed at me. "The police are here!" He squeezed under the stairs with me just as the policeman dropped through the window into the basement and turned on his flashlight. Terrified, Paulo and I froze as the policeman headed straight towards the stairs! Fortunately, he was concentrating on the fake bloody footprints and didn't notice Paulo and me as he tiptoed up the steps.

Following the trail of footprints, the policeman discovered the message on the wall above the window. As he leaned closer to read it, Gordon crept up on the man, and thinking he was just a big kid in a police costume, he reached out to push him out of the window. Gordon's hand suddenly froze in midair as he caught sight of the waistband of the kid's underwear sticking out above his pants. Not being able to resist, Gordon reached out and grabbed the underwear, giving them a good firm yank

62

before pushing him out the window. Hearing the policeman shouting, Paulo and I rushed up the stairs.

"RUN FOR IT! IT'S THE COPS!!" we shouted and took off down the stairs. We climbed out the basement window and tore off across the backyard, relieved to see that Gordon was following us.

The three of us ran until we reached the school yard, where we figured it was safe to stop and catch our breath. Quickly we explained to Gordon what had just happened.

Gordon laughed out loud. "You mean I just gave a wedgie to a cop?!"

Before we could respond, we were blinded by the headlights from three police cars as they roared into the school yard and surrounded us. Gordon, Paulo and I were quickly herded into three separate cars where we were questioned over and over. We all told the same story about wanting to raise money for charity and that Gordon didn't know that the last "kid" through our haunted house was really a cop! Paulo had the jar of money as evidence of our attempted good deed. Fortunately, the police admire people who raise money for charity and they weren't too angry at us. Even the policeman who had received the wedgie from Gordon forgave him when he saw how much money we raised. Much to our surprise, we were let off with a warning to stay away from the abandoned house, which we solemnly promised to do.

On the way home, Paulo insisted that this was the last Halloween he was going to spend with Gordon.

"Yeah," I agreed. "This is the third Halloween in a row that we've spent with the police!" But we changed our minds on Monday when it was announced that our class, which had raised the most money for charity, was going to be treated to a pizza party. Maybe Halloween with Gordon wasn't so bad after all.

Chapter 8

Mr. Lima's Bad Day

February was one of the coldest months on record in our town. We hadn't had so much snow and such cold temperatures in a century, and I wasn't looking forward to today's outing. Gordon, Paulo and I were going to spend the entire day outside trying to take pictures of a great-horned owl for a school project, and Paulo's dad had offered to drive us out to the country to a spot where we knew some owls lived. We hoped to capture some really good pictures of a great-horned owl, and maybe even a short video clip of an owl in flight. Mrs. Hoagsbrith had given our class a choice between a written assignment and a photo essay, and Gordon, Paulo and I knew which assignment we preferred.

"A thousand word essay or some pictures of a great-horned owl?" Gordon had said. "No contest!" Paulo and I had agreed whole-heartedly. That's why I was waiting at Gordon's house at 9:00 am on Saturday morning for Paulo and his dad to pick us up. We were both bundled up in our parkas and toques and two pairs of mittens to guard against the cold. When Mr. Lima's van pulled into the driveway, we wasted no time in getting into it. To our surprise, the temperature inside the van was no warmer than the temperature outside. Paulo sat beside his father shivering in the front seat, and then I noticed the open window beside Mr. Lima.

"It's a great day, huh, boys?" said Paulo's dad, his breath coming out in clouds. "It's practically spring! You can smell it in the air."

I threw a puzzled glance at Gordon. Had Mr. Lima gone crazy? It was freezing outside. Then I saw it – the hat. Mr. Lima was wearing his expensive, toasty warm beaver fur hat. Mr. Lima loved wearing his hat almost as much as he loved bragging about his hat.

"Yup," said Mr. Lima to no one in particular. "It's a great day to take pictures, especially when you're dressed for the outdoors." Paulo turned and rolled his eyes at us.

Twenty minutes later we arrived, shivering, at the edge of the woods. We climbed out of the van, gathered up our gear and started off.

"Have you got the bait?" I asked Paulo.

"Right here," he said, removing a small toy mouse and some fishing line from his pocket.

"I don't think that cat toy is going to fool any owl," said Gordon skeptically.

"Sure it will," replied Paulo. "Just wait and see. We'll put the toy mouse down on the snow and attach this fishing line to it. Then we'll hide in the bushes and every once in a while, we'll tug on the fishing line. That'll make it look like the mouse is moving. Sooner or later, a great-horned owl will spot our mouse and think it's a *real* mouse. He'll swoop down to catch it, and we'll be ready with our cameras to capture it all on film."

The plan sounded simple enough. We placed the fake mouse in the center of a small clearing, close enough to the bushes so we could get some good pictures of the owl as it swooped down on its prey. Then we crawled into the bushes to wait.

Half an hour went by and nothing happened.

"I can't feel my toes," I said, stamping my feet to get the blood flowing.

"And I think I have frostbite," said Paulo, blowing on his fingers to warm them up.

"Your dad sure looks warm," commented Gordon. We glanced over to where Mr. Lima sat on a fallen log, looking nice and warm.

Another half hour crept by and still there was no sign of an owl. I was getting cramped and cold and ready to give up when Mr. Lima announced that he was going to stretch his legs. Getting up, he paced back and forth across the small clearing. At that same instant, a great-horned owl flew out of its hiding spot in one of the trees and made straight for the clearing.

"Get your camera ready!" I whispered excitedly to Gordon. "Here it comes!"

The owl dove into the clearing, its wings spread out more than a metre wide. I could see its sharp talons ready to grab its prey, and then it happened. The owl completely ignored our fake mouse and made straight for Mr. Lima, who, with his back turned, didn't see it coming. The owl dove at the man and snatched his expensive beaver fur hat right off his head!

"Hey!" shouted Mr. Lima, turning around to see the owl fly away with his hat and land at the top of a tall poplar tree.

"My hat!" shouted Mr. Lima. "That d#@*) bird stole my hat!"

"This is great!" exclaimed Gordon, who was using his camera to videotape the scene, while Paulo was busy snapping pictures with his own camera. Mr. Lima continued to curse and shake his fist at the owl, who had deposited the hat in the crook of one of the highest branches at least five metres above our heads.

69

"Which one of you boys is going to climb that tree and get my hat back?" demanded Mr. Lima, as if the whole thing had been our fault. Gordon, Paulo and I glanced at each other. The tree was very tall and very spindly. None of the branches near the top would have supported our weight. What's more, the hat was being heavily guarded by a very large great-horned owl who thought he had just caught the world's biggest mouse.

"Dad, there's no way that tree will hold our weight," said Paulo. "Besides, I don't think that owl will give up your hat too easily. He might attack us!"

"You're right," sighed Mr. Lima. We'll have to find another way to get my hat down."

"I have an idea," said Gordon. "That owl's bound to realize that the hat isn't something he can eat. Why don't we just wait until he flies away, and then we can get our fishing rods and try casting into the tree for your hat?"

"It's worth a try," said Mr. Lima thoughtfully. "Besides, it sure is getting cold out."

Since we didn't have a better plan, we decided to head

home for our fishing rods.

It took about an hour to go home, pick up our rods and return to the woods. As we neared the clearing, we were startled to hear shotgun blasts. We jogged the rest of the way to the clearing and saw several men in hunting outfits standing around what looked like a small dead animal in the middle of the clearing.

"Hey, that's no raccoon!" we heard one of the hunters say.

"But what is it?" asked another hunter. Our eyes immediately travelled to the top of the poplar tree. There was no sign of the hat!

"My hat!" shouted Mr. Lima as we all rushed into the clearing. "You've ruined it!" he said, staring down at the bits of singed fur that had once been a very expensive beaver fur hat.

"We thought it was a raccoon!" explained one of the hunters by way of apology.

"Yeah. We're real sorry," said another. Mr. Lima just stood there, too shocked to say anything.

*　*　*　*　*

A week later, Mrs. Hoagsbrith handed back our photo essay and video clip of the great-horned owl.

"Your pictures of the owl attacking that hat were excellent," she told us. "And your video was so funny, I showed it to all the teachers in the staff room. Everyone agreed that your assignment deserves an 'A+'!"

Chapter 9

The Fire

If there was one thing our principal, Mr. Evans, always stressed, it was the importance of fire safety. Danglemore Public School had more fire drills than any other school around, and during the drill, Mr. Evans would run around with a stopwatch, a whistle and a clipboard, hollering instructions, taking head counts and timing us. When the drill was over, he would check the stopwatch and grin proudly, because nothing made our principal happier than a good fire drill. At the end of the school year, we would have an assembly and the local fire chief would present Mr. Evans with a fire safety trophy for the most fire-safe school in town. The trophy would go into the trophy case with all the other fire safety trophies. Our school didn't have many sports or academic trophies, but we sure had a lot of fire safety trophies! We students knew how important these trophies were to the teachers and the principal, so we always worked hard to win.

From the first day we had entered Junior Kindergarten, we were taught the Four Golden Rules of Fire Safety:

1. *Stop.* Stop everything you're doing when you hear the fire alarm and get quickly and quietly in line at the door.
2. *Drop.* If you see smoke, drop to the floor and crawl so the smoke doesn't get in your eyes and lungs.
3. *Roll.* In the event that you are on fire, roll around on the floor to put out the fire.
4. *Do Not Hide.* Never hide in a closet or washroom. If you see a firefighter, run towards him, never away from him.

Grade after grade, year after year, Mr. Evans made sure that our teachers taught us these rules. Nothing in our school was more important than fire safety. If a kid got a detention, he had to write out the four rules 100 times.

We knew that we were the safest and smartest school in the country when it came to fire safety. Fortunately, in the history of our school, there had never actually been a fire...until today.

After morning recess, our teacher told us that in addition to having our eyes tested, our teeth checked, and our flu shots, we were now going to have our hearing tested. The hearing test was to take place in the library. The library was the quietest spot in the school, so what we were supposed to hear, I don't know. We trooped down to the library and saw that headphones had been placed on all the tables, one pair for each of us. The windows and doors had been sealed to keep any noise out. The idea was that we would put on the headphones and listen to various sounds, and mark down what we heard on a worksheet in front of us. The test sounded simple and painless. Mrs. Hoagsbrith decided to have her ears tested along with the rest of us, and that is why none of us heard the fire alarm.

Halfway through the hearing test, a fire was

accidentally started by a workman trying to fix something in the storage room. The school's supply of art paper caught on fire. Smoke and flames billowed out into the hallway. While the rest of the school from JK to Grade 8 was executing a very orderly, well-practised evacuation, our class sat in the silent library listening to beeps and hums through our headphones. We heard and smelled nothing.

Glancing up from my worksheet, I was surprised to see smoke in the hallway outside the library. I reached over and poked Paulo with my pencil. He looked up, saw the smoke, and poked Gordon with his pencil. Looking up, Gordon saw the smoke and leaned over and poked our teacher, very gently, with *his* pencil.

Mrs. Hoagsbrith is an experienced teacher, well into her 40s or maybe even her 50s. She has taught for over 25 years, and nothing surprises her anymore. She rarely gets excited and hardly ever raises her voice. She tends to sigh a lot and roll her eyes, but that's about as worked up as she gets. When she saw the smoke, however, she jumped up and waved her arms to get our attention. Everyone saw the smoke and removed their headphones. We could hear the fire alarm ringing loudly, but fortunately, there was no panic, because if there was one thing we knew, it was fire safety.

"There's too much smoke for us to try and escape now," said our teacher. "But let's not forget our fire safety rules. We'll just have to wait to be rescued by the fire department."

We heard the blare of the fire trucks as they raced into the schoolyard, and then the sound of the firefighters' voices as they called instructions to each other. We sat calmly in the library knowing that Mr. Evans, clipboard in hand, would inform the fire chief that our class had not evacuated the building. We were confident that any second now, a whole team of professional firefighters would burst through the door to get us out.

A few minutes passed, and still we sat there, trapped in the library. We started to glance around nervously. Surely Mr. Evans had done a head count and come up 26 heads short! Where were our rescuers?

All of a sudden, the door to the library burst open, and a lone firefighter strode confidently into the room. And then it happened. Every kid in the class suddenly and at the exact same moment remembered Fire Safety Rule #4: *When You See A Firefighter, Run Towards Him.* Before the poor firefighter knew what hit him, he was buried under an avalanche of students! Mrs. Hoagsbrith was shocked. Before she could order us to get off the struggling firefighter, the fire chief came down the hall shouting that the fire was out. Noticing the boots of the firefighter sticking out from under a pile of kids, he shook his head angrily.

"Firefighter O'Connor! Quit playing with those kids! I told you to tell everyone that the fire is out, and to evacuate the building until the smoke clears!"

We climbed off the firefighter and he slowly sat up, looking dazed and stunned.

"But...but..." he stammered. Then he rolled his eyes and let out a loud sigh.

Mrs. Hoagsbrith looked at him sympathetically and said, "You're lucky. You just have to save them. I have to *teach* them!"

*   *   *   *   *

Danglemore Public School did not win the Fire Safety Trophy that year. Mr. Evans looked deeply saddened as he announced our loss to the entire school at the year-end assembly. It was also the last time that we had our hearing tested at school.

Chapter 10

Tales from the Toilet

On Monday morning, first period, Mrs. Hoagsbrith gave us a writing assignment. We were to write a short story about our most embarrassing moment. When everyone was done, we had to stand up at the front of the room and read our stories to the rest of the class. Of course, not everyone's story was that funny or even very embarrassing, until we got to Gordon's story. When Gordon finished reading, even our teacher was chuckling.

Gordon stood at the front of the room and read his story aloud to the class.

"This weekend, my parents took my sister and me to

the movies. I ordered an extra-large drink and a large tub of popcorn, so naturally, just as we were getting to the good part in the movie, I had to go to the bathroom. I just couldn't wait.

"Well," continued Gordon, "I went into the bathroom and found an empty stall. I locked the door and sat down. At the same time, a man entered the stall next to mine. A couple of seconds later he said *'Hello. How's it going?'* 'Pretty good,' I answered. 'How are you?' *'Fine, fine,'* he said. *'What are you up to?'* 'Not much,' I answered. (I mean, really, what did he think I was up to?) 'How about yourself?' I asked, just to be polite. *'I've got two tickets to the big baseball game tomorrow. You interested?'* 'Well, first I'll have to ask my parents,' I told him. And then it happened. The man said in an angry voice, *'Dave, I'll have to phone you back. I'm in the washroom, and every time I ask you a question, some stupid kid in the next stall answers and I can hardly hear you!'*

"And that," concluded Gordon, "was my most embarrassing moment."

About the Authors

Michael Wade was born a long time ago, in a place far, far away. He grew up in London, Ontario and currently lives in Strathroy, Ontario. Michael enjoys hunting, wilderness canoeing and working out.

Laura Wade was born not quite so long ago and not as far away as Michael. She, too, was raised in London, Ontario and currently resides in Strathroy, where she works as a Children's Librarian.